This edition published in 1990 by Gallery Books,
an imprint of W. H. Smith Publishers, Inc.,
112 Madison Avenue, New York, NY 10016

ISBN 0-8317-4910-5

Gallery Books are available for bulk purchase
for sales promotions and premium use.
For details write or telephone the Manager of
Special Sales, W. H. Smith Publishers, Inc.,
112 Madison Avenue, New York, NY 10016.
(212) 532 6600

Typeset by Best-Set Typesetter Ltd, Hong Kong
Printed and bound in Singapore

SNOW WHITE
AND OTHER FAIRY TALES

ILLUSTRATED BY RENE CLOKE

GALLERY BOOKS
An Imprint of W. H. Smith Publishers Inc.

"IT'S JUST AN ORDINARY ROSE!"

CONTENTS

SNOW WHITE

WHEN you prick your finger, you can make a wish. The Queen remembered this one snowy winter's day, when she pricked her finger with the needle she was sewing with. So she made a wish.

"I wish I had a beautiful baby daughter," she said to herself. This was what she longed for more than anything else in the world. Her wish came true, and a little girl was born. She had jet-black hair, blood-red lips, eyes as blue as sapphires and skin as white as snow,

THEN SHE MADE A WISH

so she was called Snow White.

Sadly, while the little Princess was still a baby, the Queen died, and before very long her father married again.

Snow White's stepmother was beautiful, but she was also vain. She loved to gaze at her reflection in the mirror. In fact she secretly kept a magic mirror that talked to her. Every day she asked it:

"Mirror, mirror on the wall
Who is the fairest of us all?"

Each time the mirror would reply:

"Oh Lady Queen, so grand and tall,
Thou art fairest of them all."

The answer was always the same – until one day, when the Princess was nine years old. On that day the Queen had a terrible shock.

By then people had noticed that Snow White was growing up to be very beauti-

SHE ALWAYS ASKED THE SAME QUESTION

ful. And when the Queen spoke to her mirror that day, it replied:

"Oh Lady Queen, thou still art fair,
But none to Snow White can compare."

The Queen immediately went into a terrible rage. And while the King was out hunting, she ordered a servant to take the little Princess into the forest and to kill her.

The servant did not dare to disobey the Queen, and he took Snow White away. But when she begged him to spare her life, he let her go.

Later, he swore to the Queen she was dead. After all, how could a little girl survive on her own, lost in the forest?

And that was what the Queen told Snow White's father when he returned. He was heartbroken, but the wicked Queen smiled at herself in the mirror.

She did not need to ask it any questions now her stepdaughter was gone!

But, deep in the forest, Snow White was still alive. She wandered along, eating berries and picking flowers. Just

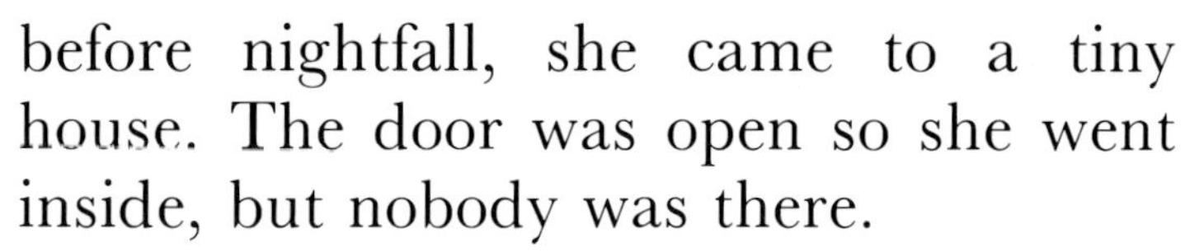

before nightfall, she came to a tiny house. The door was open so she went inside, but nobody was there.

It was the strangest little house, very untidy, and she could tell that quite a lot of very small people lived there. On the table were seven dirty little bowls, seven greasy spoons and seven mugs that needed washing!

There was some stew left in a pot on the stove. It smelled delicious and made Snow White feel very hungry.

"Perhaps whoever lives here would forgive me for eating it up if I washed the dishes for them," she thought.

In fact, she cleaned and tidied the whole house. She rather enjoyed playing house. But there were no less than seven sets of clothes to fold and seven tiny beds to make. She began to feel so tired that she lay down across them and fell asleep.

When Snow White awoke, she was startled to find seven little men around her, all staring at her intently.

"Don't be afraid, little girl, we won't harm you," said one of the dwarfs. "But

SHE DISCOVERED A TINY HOUSE

what are you doing in our house?"

Snow White told them how she had been left in the forest by the wicked Queen's servant. The dwarfs were horrified. They all adored the beautiful little girl, and promised to keep her safe if she would cook and clean for them in return.

Snow White lived with the dwarfs happily for many months. Then one day, a gypsy knocked at the door selling ribbons and laces. Before Snow White could stop her, the gypsy had tied a new lace into Snow White's dress – but much too tightly!

Snow White could hardly breathe, and fell down in a faint. For it was not a gypsy, but the jealous Queen in disguise. Vain as ever, she had asked her mirror to tell her how beautiful she was and had been furious at the reply:

"Oh lady Queen so tall and fair
Still cannot with Snow White
compare."

The Queen had screamed at the mirror, threatening to break it if it did not tell her where Snow White was. The mirror told the Queen:

"Deep within the forest glen

She dwells with seven little men."

And that's how Snow White's hiding place was discovered. Luckily, the dwarfs came back from their work in the gold mines just in time to rescue Snow White. They loosened the laces and she recovered.

"Never let any strangers into the house," they told her.

But once again the Queen learned from her mirror that Snow White still lived. This time she called at the cottage dressed as an old woman with a basket of apples to give away.

Snow White did not ask her in, but politely took the apple the old woman offered her. It was poisoned! The moment she took a bite, she fell to the ground.

When the dwarfs found Snow White, they all wept bitterly and could not bear to lose her for ever. They built a glass case for her, which stood in a lovely, sunny part of the forest, not far from the house.

For seven years the dwarfs visited her

"TASTE ONE OF THESE, MY DEAR"

every day, just to gaze at her beautiful face, which never changed.

One day, a handsome young Prince came riding through the forest and came upon them by surprise.

As soon as he saw Snow White, he fell in love with her beauty. Thinking she was asleep, he bent down to gaze at her soft skin.

"Stop, stop!" cried the dwarfs, struggling to stop the prince from touching Snow White.

By accident, the glass case was jolted and shaken. Then, to everyone's amazement, Snow White slowly opened her eyes and smiled at them, just as if she had woken from a long sleep.

When the glass case was jolted, a piece of poison apple that was stuck in Snow White's throat had been dislodged. The enchantment was broken, and she was alive and well again.

Snow White fell in love with the Prince, and soon they were married. She had seven pages at her wedding,

HE FELL IN LOVE WITH SNOW WHITE

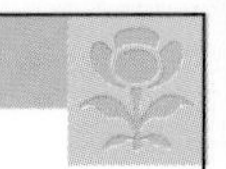

and remained friends with the dwarfs for ever.

One day soon after this, the Queen asked her mirror:

"Mirror, mirror on the wall,
Aren't I the fairest of them all?"

And the mirror replied:

"Fair you were, my Lady Queen,
But fairer now Snow White doth seem."

At this news, the Queen went mad with rage and smashed the mirror into a thousand tiny pieces.

AND SO THEY WERE MARRIED

ALI BABA AND THE FORTY THIEVES

LONG ago in the land of Arabia there lived two brothers called Ali Baba and Kassim. One day, Ali Baba was collecting firewood when he heard men on horses coming. Quickly he hid behind a tree. He noticed their fierce weapons and heavy sacks. These men must be thieves!

Suddenly the leader shouted, "Open, Sesame!" and immediately a huge rock nearby swung open like a door. All the men disappeared inside, one by one.

Ali Baba counted forty of them. In a short while, the men trooped out.

"Shut, Sesame!" cried the leader, and the rock door swung closed. Then the band of men mounted their horses and galloped away.

As soon as the men were out of sight, Ali Baba went up to the rock and tried the words for himself. “Open, Sesame!”

The door in the rock opened, and Ali Baba peered into the cave behind it. The sight that met his eyes was dazzling, for the cave was full of treasure: sacks and chests full of gold, silver and sparkling precious jewels.

Ali Baba quickly filled his sack with gold, then he hurried home to his wife and told her about his adventure.

“How much gold is there?” she asked. They began to count it.

“This will take all night, there is so much. Let’s weigh it instead,” his wife suggested. “I’ll go and borrow some scales from brother Kassim’s wife.”

“Whatever can Ali Baba have found?” wondered Kassim’s greedy wife.

To find out, she decided to put some wax on the scales. Whatever was being weighed would leave a mark or stick to the wax.

Kassim's wife was astonished to find a piece of gold stuck in the wax when

THE CAVE WAS FULL OF TREASURE

Ali Baba's wife returned the scales.

"You must ask your brother where he found so much gold that it fills up my scales," she ordered Kassim.

Her husband was as lazy as she was greedy. But he could not resist the idea of getting his hands on more gold, even though he was already quite rich.

He strolled down the street to his brother's house and saw the gold for himself. Ali Baba was feeling very happy at becoming rich so suddenly. He was pleased to share his good luck with his brother. As soon as it got dark, Ali Baba showed Kassim the cave of treasure with its secret door.

"All you have to remember is the secret password," Ali Baba explained.

"Open, Sesame! Think of sesame seeds and you won't forget it," Ali

Baba suggested to his brother.

But Kassim wasn't listening. He was already trying to think of a way to get rid of Ali Baba.

Kassim could not wait to get some of the treasure for himself. As soon as he and Ali Baba parted, he hurried back to

the cave. He let himself in and shut the rock door behind him. But Kassim spent too long filling his sacks with treasure. By the time he was ready to leave, he had forgotten the password.

"It was something to do with seeds," he said to himself. He tried "Open, Barley," then "Open, Poppy," "Open, Mustard" . . . but none of them worked.

Then he heard the sound of horses outside. The forty thieves had returned, and they caught Kassim redhanded. Furious at having their secret hideout discovered, they attacked and killed him with their swords.

When Kassim failed to return home, his anxious wife went to Ali Baba's house to ask if they had seen him. She never imagined he was already dead.

Ali Baba guessed that something

terrible had happened, and he went straight to the cave. Sadly, he brought his brother's body home and arranged a funeral. The thieves discovered that the

body was missing. Then they knew that there was someone still alive who knew the secret of their hideaway.

The leader ordered one of the men to find out where the funeral was taking place and then to put a cross on the door. But Ali Baba's clever wife noticed the cross. She quickly put crosses on all the other doors on the street.

When the thieves came to kill their enemy, they could not find the right house. They were furious at being tricked and sent out spies to find Ali Baba.

Kassim's widow had been telling everyone about Ali Baba's gold, and the thieves found out. The leader worked out a plan to smuggle all his men right into the courtyard of Ali Baba's house so they could all jump out and attack him. The leader bought a string of donkeys and some large jars. One was filled with oil, and the rest had men hidden inside. Then he arrived at Ali Baba's house, claiming to be a long-lost friend of the family. He was invited to unload the donkeys and to leave all the jars in the

courtyard. This was exactly as he had planned it.

Ali Baba's wife was very suspicious and pretended she needed some oil. When she knocked on the first jar to see how full it was, she was surprised to hear a voice inside whisper, "Is it time for us to fight yet?"

"No, not yet," she replied quickly. She went around all the jars, saying the same thing.

When she found the jar full of oil, she put it to boil on the fire.

Then she poured some of the scalding oil into each jar. When the leader gave the signal for the attack, no one came. All his men were dead, and he was on his own. The leader of the thieves ran for his life. Thanks to his quick-thinking wife, Ali Baba's life was saved.

After a year had passed Ali Baba went back to the cave. He stood before the huge rock and said "Open, Sesame." The door opened and he went in to discover all the treasure still there. He took enough for he and his wife to live happily and returned home knowing his secret was safe.

HIS WIFE OUTSMARTED THE THIEVES

THE SWINEHERD

A HANDSOME prince fell in love with the Emperor's daughter. But she was a very spoiled Princess who had everything a young girl could want, and he knew she would be hard to win. The Prince was not rich, and all he could think of to give her were the two most precious things he owned.

One was a rose which flowered over his father's grave. It had only a single perfect bloom once every five years. The other was a nightingale that sang the most beautiful tunes in the world.

HE PLUCKED THE WONDERFUL ROSE

The prince sent the gifts to the palace in two handsome silver chests. There was great excitement when they arrived. But when they were opened, the spoiled Princess was disappointed.

"It's just an ordinary rose," she complained, looking in the first chest. "And what a dull little brown bird! Let it fly away," she ordered sulkily, turning her back on the second chest.

The Prince heard how ungraciously the Princess had received his gifts.

"I'll teach that young lady a lesson before I marry her," he decided.

The next day, he put on a tattered cloak and a battered old hat and went to the palace. He knocked at the door and pretended he was looking for work.

"Is that another Prince bringing presents?" asked the greedy Princess

THE GIFTS ARRIVED IN SILVER CHESTS

hopefully, when she heard him knock.

"No, Your Highness," the footman told her. "It's only a poor man looking for work. I sent him down to the pigsty because we need a new swineherd." So the Prince became a swineherd and looked after the pigs.

To cook his food he used a little pot which had bells hung around it. When the pot boiled, the bells played a tune. It was also a magic pot! Whoever sniffed it could smell what was cooking in all the houses all over town.

The servants began gossiping about the swineherd with his amazing pot, and the Princess grew curious.

"Tell the swineherd I will give him a gold coin if he will give me the magic pot. It would be such fun to have as a plaything," she said to her maid.

The maid went to the dirty old pigsty and gave the swineherd the message. But the swineherd shook his head.

"Tell the Princess that I don't want

money, but she can have the pot if she will give me ten kisses," he said.

The maid was horrified at the idea and hardly dared to repeat the swineherd's answer to the Princess. But the young man insisted that was his price, so the Princess finally agreed.

"You must all stand around so nobody can see," she told her maids.

The Emperor, who was on his way to see the famous pot for himself, noticed the crowd of girls by the pigsty. When he saw his daughter kissing the swineherd, he was furious.

"Leave me immediately," he roared, and banished them both from his kingdom to a place where it poured with rain and the miserable Princess was always drenched.

"Whatever shall I do?" she wailed. "I

"I DEMAND TEN KISSES FOR THE POT"

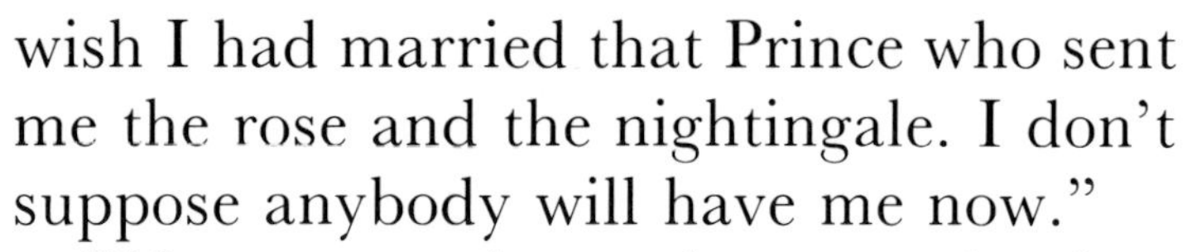

wish I had married that Prince who sent me the rose and the nightingale. I don't suppose anybody will have me now."

"If you promise to be a much nicer person from now on," said the swineherd, "I can make your wish come true."

The Princess was about to protest in her usual haughty way, when she turned and saw, not a swineherd, but the Prince himself. He had thrown away his old hat and cloak and was smiling down at her. Despite all her faults he still loved her and wanted to marry her. The Princess learned to be humble and kind by following her husband's example, and they both lived happily ever after.

"I CAN MAKE YOUR WISH COME TRUE"